NEPTUNE ADVENTURES

#6 RED TIDE ALERT

Other
NEPTUNE ADVENTURES
by Susan Saunders
from Avon Camelot

(#1) DANGER ON CRAB ISLAND
(#2) DISASTER AT PARSONS POINT
(#3) THE DOLPHIN TRAP
(#4) STRANDING ON CEDAR POINT
(#5) HURRICANE RESCUE

#6 RED TIDE ALERT

SUSAN SAUNDERS

This is a work of fiction. Names, characters, places, and incidents either are the product of the author's imagination or are used fictitiously. Any resemblance to actual events, locales, organizations, or persons, living or dead, is entirely coincidental and beyond the intent of either the author or the publisher.

AVON BOOKS, INC.
1350 Avenue of the Americas
New York, New York 10019

Published by arrangement with the author
Visit our website at **http://www.AvonBooks.com**
ISBN: 0-380-80253-8

First Avon Camelot Printing: December 1998

CAMELOT TRADEMARK REG. U.S. PAT. OFF. AND IN OTHER COUNTRIES, MARCA REGISTRADA, HECHO EN U.S.A.

Printed in the U.S.A.

OPM 10 9 8 7 6 5 4 3 2 1

To Abby McAden, with thanks
for her help and encouragement.

CHAPTER ONE

''Gross!'' Tyler Chapin said, wrinkling his nose.

He was standing on the metal platform at the top of the Parsons Point lighthouse with his cousin Dana, looking down at a sandy beach littered with the still bodies of fish. Each wave that washed ashore deposited dozens more of them—dead sea trout and sea bass and perch.

''First a red tide kills little fish—the poison from the algae paralyzes their breathing—then bigger fish and sea turtles and birds that eat the fish, like seagulls and ospreys, on up to young seals and dolphins, even foxes that grab dead fish off the beaches,'' Dana Chapin said gloomily. ''We'll have to keep an eye on Jake, too,'' she added. Jake was Dana's yellow Lab.

Tyler stared farther out into Badger Bay, usually a sparkling blue-green in the bright sunlight. That morning large patches of water were stained a murky reddish-brown, colored by the microscopic bodies of poisonous algae that were multiplying by the second.

"It's like some kind of weird sci-fi movie," Tyler said, glancing at the drifts of dead fish on the beach below. "Why does it happen? And how long does it last?"

"Nobody ever knows how long," Dana said, "or even exactly why it starts. It's a bad combination of sunny weather, warm water temperatures, and fertilizers and sewage that end up in the ocean. Red tides can last for weeks."

"If we need to take in more animals because of the red tide," Tyler said, his thoughts jumping ahead to the consequences, "where are we going to put them all?"

"Yeah, we're definitely running out of room," Dana agreed uneasily.

Dana's parents, Tyler's Uncle Joe and Aunt Lissa, had founded Project Neptune thirteen years earlier, to rescue sick and stranded marine mammals and sea turtles, nurse them back to health, and release them again into the wild. There was a lot of space for recovering animals inside the huge stranding barn, across the gravel road from the lighthouse. Wire cages for seals lined its walls. Three large fiberglass tanks for them to swim in stood in the center of the floor.

But Neptune had had a busy summer this year, winding up with a full-scale hurricane that had brought in even more patients. The stranding barn was full to bursting already.

Tyler started counting in his head. *Nine harbor seals in the barn right now, a grey seal, three harp seals, two pilot whales in the outdoor tank, a little hooded seal and a young grey seal in the vet clinic. . . .*

"Dana—Tyler!" Aunt Lissa called from downstairs. "Ten minutes till your bus gets here."

"Coming!" Dana called back. As they started down the iron steps that wound around the inside of the two-hundred-year-old tower, she asked Tyler, "Did you study for the science test?"

"Yeah, for an hour, at least," Tyler said.

Eighth grade had barely gotten off the ground at Rockport Middle School, but Tyler had already had major homework, not to mention several pop quizzes. He could have done without an exam in science as well. Besides, he would have liked to use some of his class time that day to ask Mr. Foley, the science teacher, more about red tides.

Mr. Foley had been a Neptuner for years. That's what the volunteers at Project Neptune called themselves. He knew about everything that went on in the bays and coves around Parsons Point. Tyler had lived in Fairbanks, Alaska, all of his life—he'd only been staying with his uncle, aunt, and cousin since last January—so red tide was a totally new experience for him.

Tyler and Dana said good-bye to Aunt Lissa. She was in the kitchen, mixing up a tonic of vitamins and medicines for a young hooded seal, while Jake snoozed in the corner. The cousins grabbed their backpacks off the table. As soon as they stepped out onto the back porch, Tyler's nose started to itch.

''That might be the red tide,'' Dana told him after he'd sneezed a couple of times. ''Waves push drops of poison into the air, and the wind carries them inland. For people with allergies . . .''

''I doubt it. I'm never allergic to anything,'' Tyler said, sneezing again.

The cousins headed across the gravel road for a quick visit to the outdoor tank before they met their school bus.

''Summer before last,'' Dana said, ''just breathing near a red tide made Bonnie Bishop and some of the other Neptuners sick. We couldn't go swimming or kayaking, and—''

''What about the fish for our animals to eat?'' Tyler interrupted.

The marine mammals recuperating at Project Neptune feasted on hundreds of pounds of fish daily, much of it bought from local fishermen. But with red tide polluting the waters, the fish might not be safe for them.

''We've probably got enough fish frozen in the food-prep shed for a week or so,'' Dana said. ''After that . . . Mom and Dad may have to shop farther north, someplace where there aren't any red-tide problems.''

Then she smiled. Bonnie and Claude, the two young pilot whales in the outdoor tank, had poked their heads out of the water. They were watching Tyler and Dana walk toward them.

The whales looked a lot like dark-skinned dolphins, only larger: Claude weighed close to a thousand pounds and was ten feet long, Bonnie a little shorter. She suddenly leaped high into the air and smacked down sideways on the surface of the pool with a giant splash.

Claude had to be more cautious because of his torn fore flipper, ripped by wooden debris during the hurricane. The edges of the wound had been sewn back together and Claude was healing, but he was still sore. He whistled loudly, though, and circled the tank at a fast clip.

''Claude's raring to go,'' someone murmured from behind Tyler. It was Uncle Joe, in the rubber boots Neptuners wore to clean out the tanks in the stranding barn.

''How much longer until the whales'll be released?'' Tyler whispered. He'd lowered his voice, too. The wild animals at the Point weren't supposed to get too used to humans beings, not even to the sound of their voices.

''We'll have to wait and see,'' Uncle Joe whispered back. ''Several more months, at least.''

Several more months could mean November, or even December, which was when Tyler would be leaving the Point himself. He'd been trying not to think about it too much, but the fact was always there, lurking at the back of his mind.

Tyler's dad, Jim Chapin, was a biologist like Uncle Joe and Aunt Lissa, but he worked with land animals instead of sea mammals. He'd gotten a grant to study wolves in the Canadian Arctic for a year, so he'd sent

Tyler to stay with his Atlantic Coast relatives for that time.

At first, Tyler could hardly wait to get back to Fairbanks. He'd been miserably homesick for his dad and his friends and Thane, his malamute. And for Alaska itself. He'd had a new school and a whole group of new kids to deal with, plus he and Dana had had to make some major adjustments in their daily lives. They hadn't seemed to have much in common besides their last name. And both of them had been used to being the only kid in their households.

Now that Tyler had been at the Point for nine months, though, he was looking forward to leaving it less and less. He was really into helping out at Project Neptune. He'd made some cool friends in Rockport. And he'd started to like having another kid around all the time, to talk to and do things with—even to argue with.

Back in January, Tyler never could have guessed that it might be just as hard to leave Parsons Point as it had been to come here in the first place.

Uncle Joe put his arms around Tyler and Dana's shoulders and walked them farther away from the whales. "We need a plan for your mom's birthday," he said to Dana. "It's getting close, and it's an important one."

Tyler knew that Aunt Lissa would be forty years old at the end of the next week.

"Before this red tide, I'd been thinking that we might have a big clambake on the bay beach and invite all the

Neptuners,'' Uncle Joe went on. ''But piles of dead fish aren't exactly festive. And we wouldn't be able to eat the clams, either. So that's out.''

''What about an overnight trip?'' Dana suggested. ''Like to Wilton or even to Newport? You and Mom could go out to dinner at a fancy restaurant, and . . .''

''I have a feeling we'll be too busy around here to take much time off,'' Uncle Joe said. ''Unless we get lucky, and the weather turns colder and the algae stop growing. . . . I hear your bus,'' he added.

Those horn blasts meant Mrs. Raynor had stopped the school bus to pick up Stephanie Marin, and would soon be rolling up Harbor Lane toward the Point.

''Anyway, think about the birthday party!'' Uncle Joe called to Tyler and Dana as they hurried down the gravel road.

''I haven't even come up with any ideas for a great gift for Mom,'' Dana said while they jogged along.

''Neither have I,'' Tyler said. ''It would make sense for us to pool our money—get her something totally outstanding together,'' he added.

''Okay, but what?'' said Dana. She went on, ''Mom needs a new pair of rubber boots. I heard her say her old boots are shredding.''

''Boring,'' said Tyler.

''Yeah, you're right. What about a windbreaker? Mom's has white spots all over it from the stranding barn,'' said Dana. Neptuners used gallons of bleach when they cleaned out cages and tanks.

''Uh-uh,'' Tyler said. ''We need to think of a birthday present way cooler than that.''

Tyler wanted to give his aunt something really special, not just because it was a major birthday for her but also because it was probably the last he'd be spending here.

''Cooler than that . . .'' Dana said. They'd reached the row of mailboxes at the edge of Harbor Lane. ''What Mom would really, really like is a bigger stranding barn.''

''So I guess we'll just knock one together ourselves,'' Tyler said, rolling his eyes.

Dana giggled. ''Yeah, easy—over the weekend,'' she said. Then she added, ''Hey, we should ride our bikes into town instead of taking the bus this morning. That way we can check out the shops on Main Street after school.''

''That's a plan,'' Tyler said.

As the yellow-and-blue school bus approached, they waved it on. Tyler and Dana ran back up the gravel road for their bikes.

CHAPTER TWO

Even though Dana was kidding about giving her mom a bigger stranding barn, she couldn't imagine anything her mother wanted more. Both her parents had been talking for years about adding another building to those already standing at the Point. But it was so expensive to feed and care for the rescued animals that Project Neptune never had a dime left over for additional expenses. Another barn would cost thousands of dollars!

At lunch in the middle-school cafeteria that day, some of the other kids tried to help out with gift suggestions. Dana's best friend, Kim Meyers, said, "I know your mom likes flowers. Why don't you plant some roses for her?"

"There's not enough soil at the Point," Dana said. "It's practically solid rock. Plus roses would probably croak in so much wind and salt spray." Parsons Point stuck straight out into the Atlantic Ocean like the prow of a boat.

Cassie Parker said, ''What about a day at House of Beauty in Wilton? Your mom could get a facial, and have her hair and nails done. . . .''

Dana and Kim grinned at each other. Cassie's mom might enjoy hanging around a beauty salon for a whole day, but Lissa Chapin would spend her time there worrying about what she could have been accomplishing at the Point.

''Thanks, but I don't think perfect hair and hands would last very long at Project Neptune,'' Dana said.

She could just imagine her mom cleaning out a seal cage, or stuffing chopped squid into a baby dolphin's mouth, with moussed hair and painted fingernails.

''Oh. Right,'' said Cassie, making a face. ''I forgot about handfuls of fish guts.'' She hated getting *her* hands dirty.

Tyler set his tray down at the far end of their table, followed by his best friends, the Mote twins. Charlie Mote was wearing his dad's old Army jacket, about ten sizes too big for him. Carter Mote's faded jeans were too short for his legs, and his blond hair was standing straight up in front—sometimes he cut it himself.

Not so long ago, Dana had thought the twins were way too grubby to even talk to, much less hang out with. But when Tyler had started being friends with them, Dana had gotten to know them better, too. She liked the Motes now, especially Carter.

Cassie obviously didn't feel the same way. Dana

heard her sigh disapprovingly when Carter slid into the empty seat next to Dana.

"Carter says he'd be glad to draw something for us to give Aunt Lissa," Tyler told Dana. "The lighthouse or harbor seals hauled out on the beach or dolphins—whatever we want."

"That's really nice of you, Carter," Dana said, smiling at him. "I think we have to come up with something for Mom on our own, though."

Then Hallie Wade sat down between Carter and Tyler. Hallie had always been a summer visitor to Rockport. But in early September, she and her mother had moved into her great-aunt Gretchen's house full-time, and Hallie had started going to Rockport Middle School. She and the Motes had known each other forever, so Hallie had gotten friendly with Tyler, too.

And she'd joined Project Neptune. Hallie could be bossy and opinionated sometimes, but she was a great Neptuner. Nobody worked harder around the stranding barn than Hallie Wade, or cared more about animals.

That day, Hallie was all upset about the red tide. "The last time there was a red tide this bad, my aunt Gretchen said dozens of sea turtles washed ashore, dead," she announced. "And most of them were Kemp's ridley turtles."

"Our dad says this tide's already killing fingerlings, which'll leave the big fish with nothing to eat," Charlie said worriedly. The twins' father was a fisherman, so the Motes had plenty to be concerned about.

‘‘My folks are working on a story about red tides for WLIR,’’ Kim said. The Meyers ran the Rockport TV station. ‘‘I saw some video they shot yesterday. There are mounds of rotting fish all over Indian Beach, and dead seagulls, too.’’

‘‘Do you mind? I do *not* need to hear about dead birds and rotten fish while I’m trying to eat my lunch!’’ Cassie exclaimed huffily. She pushed her chair back and stood up. ‘‘And as far as I’m concerned, turtles are nothing more than snakes with shells,’’ she went on. ‘‘Those long, scrawny necks—they’re totally creepy.’’

‘‘We’re talking about *Kemp’s ridleys*, Cassie,’’ Dana said. Kemp’s ridley sea turtles were so endangered that there were probably less than fifteen hundred of them left on Earth.

‘‘Even one dead ridley’s a huge loss to the whole world!’’ Hallie chimed in.

Cassie didn’t hear her. She was already marching across the room to dump her tray.

‘‘I guess Cassie is totally not interested in animals,’’ Dana murmured, not for the first time. It was so hard for Dana to imagine.

Almost everybody Dana knew had pets. And practically everyone that she was really friendly with, including Cassie’s cousin Andrew Reed, had become a Neptuner over the past few years—except Cassie. Even Charlie and Carter helped out at the Point sometimes, although their dad wasn’t exactly a big supporter of the Project.

Which made Dana wonder: *Doesn't Cassie ever feel left out?*

"You can't trust people who don't like animals," Hallie said darkly.

"Maybe Cassie's just afraid of them. She's scared of seals—she always mentions their sharp teeth," Kim pointed out. "And now we know she doesn't like sea turtles much, either. Cassie's not ever going to be a Neptuner, Dana," she added, guessing what Dana might be thinking.

"She wouldn't necessarily have to deal with the animals. She could help out on beach patrols," Dana said. Neptuners walked the beaches year-round, picking up trash so that wild animals and birds couldn't eat it or get caught in it. "It's *her* environment, too," Dana added.

"Cassie probably thinks if she recycles her soda cans, she's doing enough for *her* environment," said Tyler.

Right on cue, Cassie tossed her Coke can into the blue bin near the door. She left the cafeteria without looking back.

"Cassie will probably wear *fur* when she grows up, and sea-turtle boots!" Hallie muttered.

"So what about your mom's birthday gift?" Kim asked Dana, changing the subject. Kim never liked saying bad things about anyone. "There are some great-looking barn jackets in the Post Stop. Red canvas with a plaid wool lining."

"No clothes," Tyler said to Dana. "Clothes aren't special enough."

''Your mom likes to cook, doesn't she?'' said Hallie. ''Aunt Gertrude bought this bread-making machine that you just pour flour and a couple of other things into and it. . . .''

''It's my dad who likes to cook,'' Dana said.

''What about one of those collapsible fishing rods?'' said Charlie. ''Rockport Fuel and Bait just got in a whole shipment, and—''

''That's a lot closer to what *you* want for *your* birthday,'' Tyler said to him with a laugh.

''Anyway, we rode our bikes to school,'' Dana told them all. ''We're checking out the Main Street stores later.''

Then the bell rang, announcing that lunch was over.

Dana thought she did well on the science test that afternoon. Some of the questions were even fun, like: ''If you had all the money you needed to make a major improvement in our environment, what would it be?''

Dana wrote about cleaning up the oceans, and she wondered about Cassie's answer.

While Mr. Foley was collecting their papers, he said, ''I'd like to talk to you for a couple of minutes about red tide. Scientists are pretty certain that human beings play a large part in causing it. When we pollute the oceans with lots of chemicals and sewage, we fertilize poisonous algae and make them grow.'' Mr. Foley went on, ''Maybe someday we'll figure out how to stop polluting altogether. But right now I want to tell you what to do if you find sick birds, animals, or turtles affected by the red tide.''

Mr. Foley explained about covering the birds' heads with a towel or a jacket so they wouldn't struggle to fly away. He warned the kids not to get too close to stranded seals, because the frightened animals might hurt them. And he talked about sea turtles.

''Turtles are cold-blooded, which means their body temperature is directly influenced by the temperature of the world around them. If you find one floating in shallow water, pull it ashore so it won't drown. Then, if it's a sunny day,'' Mr. Foley said, ''look for some driftwood or seaweed to shade the turtle on the beach, to prevent it from overheating. Keep it moist with seawater, too.

''But the bottom line is, these animals will need special care to fight the poison in their systems,'' he told the class. ''So the faster you get help from Project Neptune, the more likely it is that you'll save their lives. That phone number is 555-8863.''

Mr. Foley wrote the number on the board for everyone to copy. He added, ''Stay out of the red tide yourselves. And if your eyes, nose, or throat itch or burn, or if your tongue or lips start tingling, move away from the shoreline. You're having a reaction to tiny particles of poison carried on the wind.''

As soon as school was over that afternoon, Dana and Tyler rode up Main Street on their bikes. They looked around in Lynn's Stationery and Gifts, in the Seashell Emporium, and even in Griffing Hardware, hoping to come up with a brilliant gift idea. But nothing grabbed Dana as the perfect present for her mom. Tyler didn't see anything that he really liked, either.

Discouraged, they were climbing onto their bikes again when voices yelled, "Hey, Tyler!" "Dana!" and Hallie and the Mote twins turned into Griffing's parking lot.

"What are you guys doing?" Tyler said after they'd coasted up to the bike rack.

"We've already done it," Hallie said, pointing to a brown paper bag strapped to the back of her bike. "I got some cat toys and treats for Fiona and Carter at Golding's Feed." Hallie's kittens were named for Hurricane Fiona and Carter Mote.

"We picked up a couple of packages of fishhooks for our granddad at Rockport Fuel and Bait," said Charlie.

"Did you find a birthday present for your mom?" Carter asked Dana.

Dana shook her head. "It's getting kind of depressing," she said.

"Want to come with us?" Charlie said then.

"Yeah, we're taking a look at some of the inlets," Hallie said.

"To see how far the red tide has spread out of the bay," Charlie said.

Dozens of inlets cut into the mainland around Rockport. Some were too shallow and narrow for more than a few schools of baby fish. Others were deep enough for boat traffic. All of them flowed into and out of Badger Bay.

"Good idea," Tyler said.

"Okay," said Dana.

Maybe a long bike ride was exactly what she needed—sometimes the best way to come up with an idea was *not* to think about it.

CHAPTER THREE

Tyler, Dana, Charlie, Carter, and Hallie pedaled to the far end of Main Street. Instead of taking the road out of the town, though, the Motes turned onto a narrow dirt trail that wound into a pine thicket. The rest of them followed, single file.

"I didn't know there was anything back here," Tyler said as they bounced over thick tree roots and swerved around fallen branches.

"Neither did I," said Dana.

"Yeah, our granddad used to bring us fishing for flounder," Charlie said over his shoulder.

"Wood Duck Inlet," Carter added.

"That's what it's called," said Charlie.

The trees ended suddenly, except for dozens of charred stumps on either side of the trail.

"Wow—must have been a brush fire," Hallie said.

"Yeah, a big one about five years ago," Charlie said.

"Started by lightning," said Carter.

"We haven't fished here since then," Charlie went on. "The inlet's not much farther on. . . ."

But they hadn't reached it when Tyler braked his bike. "Check that out!" he said.

A long, low building of faded bricks was surrounded by tall weeds and a few large pieces of rusted machinery.

Dana and Hallie stopped, too.

"What is this place?" Dana asked.

"It's way too big to be a house," Hallie added.

Charlie and Carter turned their bikes around and pedaled back to them.

"Granddad told us this was a boatyard when he was a kid," Charlie said. "There was once a pier on the inlet behind the building, where the boats docked for repairs. But it burned in the fire."

"Who does this belong to now?" Dana asked the twins.

"Maybe nobody," said Carter.

"It's been empty for years and years," Charlie said.

Tyler rolled his bike forward and peered through a broken window. "I'm going in," he announced.

"Yeah, let's explore!" Hallie exclaimed.

"Maybe we shouldn't," Dana said uneasily. "We could get into serious—"

"Who'll ever know?" said Hallie, leaning her bike against a stump.

Tyler found an old metal bucket in the weeds and

carried it over to the window. Hallie held the bucket steady for him to stand on.

Tyler threw one leg over the windowsill, then lowered himself to the concrete floor inside. He was standing in an open space almost as large as the big room in the stranding barn, except that the ceiling was a lot lower.

Hallie landed beside Tyler with a thump. "Wow!" she said. "We could skate in here in bad weather!" She'd gotten a new pair of inline skates for her birthday, and she was already worrying about winter.

Charlie climbed through the window, too. "It's big enough for a basketball court!" he said.

Dana and then Carter joined them.

"Maybe we could even build a couple of skate ramps . . ." Hallie was mumbling.

"Uh-uh—d'you know what this would be perfect for?" Dana asked, sounding really excited.

And Tyler was thinking the same thing. "It's Aunt Lissa's birthday present!" he said, just as Dana blurted out: "A stranding barn!"

"Her birthday present?" Carter said, puzzled, as he looked around the dark, empty room.

"You *have* a stranding barn," said Hallie.

"Project Neptune needs a lot more space. We're overcrowded already, and if this red tide lasts longer than a few days," Dana explained, "we won't have anywhere to put sick sea turtles, much less extra seals or dolphins."

"Uncle Joe and Aunt Lissa will have to start trucking

animals all the way up the coast to the stranding center at Cape Mayo,'' Tyler said. ''And if the animals are in bad shape to begin with . . .''

''They might not make it to Cape Mayo alive,'' Hallie said, understanding.

Tyler nodded. ''This place would be great!'' he said. ''It's not far from an inlet, so we could bring stranded animals in by boat. . . .''

''This building's not in such bad shape,'' Charlie said, staring upward. ''But there are a few water spots on the ceiling, which means there are some leaks in the roof.''

''It had electricity at one time,'' Hallie said, pointing to a bare lightbulb on the opposite wall.

''If the building doesn't belong to anyone, maybe the town trustees would *give* it to Project Neptune!'' said Dana.

''Like they donated the old courthouse for a senior center,'' Carter said.

''Uncle Joe might know who—'' Tyler began.

But Dana said, ''No, let's keep it a secret from Dad, too. Maybe we'll let some of the Neptuners in on it—''

''Neptuners who can do wiring and plumbing,'' said Hallie.

''And roofing,'' said Carter.

''Tim and Lou and—'' Dana began.

''We could paint it ourselves,'' Charlie interrupted.

''I'll do a mural on the walls,'' Carter said.

''It could be terrific!'' said Tyler, glancing around the

room. ''We could put two or three exercise tanks in here for seals . . .''

''And a bunch of small tanks for turtles,'' said Dana.

''I bet Granddad knows all about this place,'' Charlie said. ''We'll ask him who to talk to.''

''Phone us as soon as you find out. We need to make some serious plans,'' Tyler said.

Dana checked her watch then. ''We'd better get moving,'' she said to Tyler, ''or we'll miss feeding Bonnie and Claude.'' The cousins were in charge of serving the whales dinner every evening.

Before they left for home, though, the five kids checked out Wood Duck Inlet.

Red tide hadn't reached it yet. The water was so clear that Tyler could see horseshoe crabs resting on the sandy bottom, and small fish darting through the weeds.

''Those must be the pilings from that old pier,'' he said, pointing to a half dozen blackened logs lined up in the inlet.

''They might be solid enough to rebuild on,'' Charlie said.

As they collected their bikes, Tyler said, ''There'd be plenty of space in this building for aquariums, too. Uncle Joe and Aunt Lissa are always wishing they had room for some, to display local fish and shellfish and crabs.''

''And then we could open the place to visitors,'' Dana said. ''It would be an excellent way to get even more people interested in Project Neptune.''

“It’s a great location, practically in the middle of downtown Rockport. Everybody in town would volunteer!” said Hallie.

“Of course, a road might help,” Dana said as they dodged tree stumps on their way out.

“But we wouldn’t really need one, not at first,” Tyler said. “There’s always Wood Duck Inlet.”

“I can just see us chugging up the inlet in Lou’s Boston whaler, with a seal or a turtle for the new stranding barn,” Dana said dreamily.

“It could work,” Hallie said.

“It would be outstanding!” said Tyler.

CHAPTER FOUR

''This could be the most amazing birthday gift ever!'' Tyler said while he and Dana rode up Harbor Lane toward the Point.

''And the sooner we get going on it, the better,'' Dana said, glancing toward the edge of Badger Bay on the far side of the road. Even from this distance, Dana could see dark patches of poisonous algae coloring the water. She half expected to spot several sea turtles washing ashore, stunned by the red tide.

''Hey, there's a kid sitting on the beach,'' Tyler said suddenly, and they both braked their bikes.

A girl was kneeling on a narrow strip of sand. She seemed to be focused on something right in front of her.

''It's Stephanie Marin,'' Dana said, recognizing Stephanie's dark, curly hair. She knew Stephanie ran a couple of miles up and down Harbor Lane every day, staying in shape for the middle school field-hockey team.

"What's she looking at?" asked Tyler.

"Let's find out," Dana said. She and Tyler pushed their bikes across the road and rolled them into the beach grass on the far side.

"What's up?" Dana yelled to Stephanie above the sound of the waves.

"It's a sea turtle," Stephanie called back. "It's not moving. . . ."

The cousins dropped their bikes and ran over to her, and Dana kneeled down, too. "It's a Kemp's ridley—an adult," she said, noticing the greenish-gray color of the shell.

"It's not very big," Tyler murmured, sounding surprised, and Dana remembered he'd never seen one before.

Her cousin had seen loggerheads and green turtles, but the ridleys usually didn't start turning up on beaches near the Point until cold weather arrived in late fall. Ridleys were warm-water turtles, hatched on the coast of Mexico. If they didn't begin their return migration south early enough, the lower temperatures could stun or even kill them.

But the water in Badger Bay wasn't cold yet. This turtle had been sickened by the red tide.

"Kemp's ridleys are the smallest of the sea turtles," Dana told Tyler. "They're usually not much more than two feet across."

"It's amazing that such a little guy could swim thousands of miles every year," Tyler said.

What was amazing to Dana was the fact that these same turtles had been around for twenty or thirty million years, doing just fine. And then human beings had managed to almost wipe them off the face of the Earth in only fifty or sixty years!

This poor ridley wouldn't be making the migration—it wasn't going anywhere. Its narrow head hung loosely out of the front of the round shell. Even its tail was limp.

"It's a male," Dana said. "Females have much shorter tails."

"I've been dumping water on him with this clamshell, like Mr. Foley told us," Stephanie said, "but I think he's dead already."

When the three of them leaned forward and peered at the ridley from only inches away, though, Dana suddenly caught her breath. "His right flipper . . ." she said.

"I saw it twitch, too!" Tyler said.

The fore flipper moved again, just a fraction.

"He's alive, barely. We have to get some help from the Point right away," Dana said to Tyler.

"I'll stay here with Stephanie and keep the turtle wet," Tyler told her. "Just hurry!"

Dana grabbed her bike and pedaled as fast as she could up Harbor Lane. When she finally reached the gravel road at the Point, she spotted six or eight trucks and cars parked next to the stranding barn. Whenever there was an emergency, like during the oil spill or after the hurricane, crowds of Neptuners showed up at all hours of the day and night to care for rescued animals.

So it's starting already, Dana said to herself.

As she rolled up to the barn, Sue Larkin and Jane Hodges, both long-time Neptuners, were unloading a canvas stretcher from Sue's truck. A large turtle lay squarely in the middle of it.

"Oh, good—Dana, help us out here, okay?" Jane puffed.

Dana grabbed a stretcher handle, and she and Jane walked backward with it.

"Heavy!" Sue said breathlessly, holding on to the other end of the stretcher. "We got a call about this beached loggerhead from a man on Peggy's Cove," she told Dana.

Adult loggerheads could easily weigh two hundred pounds. They were more than twice the size of Kemp's ridleys. Maybe they were stronger than ridleys in general, or at least better able to withstand the red tide, because this loggerhead could still hold its head up. It clawed weakly at the stretcher with its front flippers, trying to escape.

Short tail: female, Dana noted, before asking, "Where are you putting her?" The women were edging carefully toward the barn with the stretcher.

"Golding's Feed lent us five rubber stock tanks for stranded turtles," Sue said, panting a little. "Three are set up in the barn and two in your house . . ."

"In the basement," Jane finished for her.

As soon as Sue, Jane, and Dana stepped into the barn, Walter McGrath and Donny Nolan, more volunteers, rushed to take the stretcher from them.

From the far end of the stranding barn, Brian Wilson yelled; "Over here!" Dana's dad and Dr. Bucalo, Neptune's veterinarian, were standing beside him.

Now Dana told Sue and Jane about the Kemp's ridley. "Tyler's with him, and Stephanie Marin, on the bay beach about halfway to Rockport," Dana said. "When I left, the turtle was hardly moving."

"Let's go!" Sue said. She grabbed another stretcher from the cabinet near the door and hurried outside to her truck.

"You'll show us where . . ." Jane added, letting Dana slide into the passenger side before she climbed in, too.

Dana didn't have to point out the spot, though. Stephanie Marin was standing next to the road, watching for them.

"How's the ridley doing?" Dana called through the truck window as soon as Sue pulled onto the shoulder of Harbor Lane.

"I can't tell. But I'm worried about Tyler," Stephanie said.

"What about Tyler?" Sue asked her, concerned.

"He's been sneezing a lot," Stephanie said. "And I think he feels sort of funny—"

"Uh-oh—red tide!" Jane exclaimed.

She and Sue scrambled out of the truck and ran down to the beach. Dana was only a few steps behind them.

Tyler was sitting next to the ridley with his legs drawn up. His chin was propped on his knees.

"Are you okay?" Jane asked him, tilting his head back to examine his face.

Dana thought Tyler's lips looked puffy, and his nose was red.

"I'm fine," Tyler said. Then he sneezed three times in a row, and admitted, "My throat and nose itch. And I'm a little . . . dizzy."

Sue took hold of one of his arms, Jane the other, and they pulled Tyler to his feet. "We're putting you in the truck right now," Sue said.

"But what about the turtle?" Tyler protested.

"Stephanie and I'll help Tyler," Dana said quickly to Sue. "You look after the ridley."

"Stick Tyler inside the truck and roll up the windows. Get him out of this wind," Sue told the girls as they walked Tyler away from the beach.

"Wow!" he murmured, stumbling over a clump of beach grass. "I feel totally bizarre."

"You'll have to be really careful and stay away from the bay," Dana said, "because the more often you're exposed to red tide, the stronger a reaction you'll get."

"I guess I'll be okay working at the *new* stranding barn," he said with a smile.

They reached the truck. Dana and Stephanie leaned Tyler against it.

''What new stranding barn?'' Stephanie asked.

''There's an old building on Wood Duck Inlet,'' Dana answered while she opened the passenger door. ''We're hoping that it doesn't belong to anyone—get in, Tyler—and that the town trustees will let Project Neptune use it.''

''Because we have more animals than we have room,'' Tyler said from the front seat.

''I'm closing the door,'' Dana told him.

''I can ask my mom about the building,'' Stephanie said to Dana. ''She works at the courthouse, where all the property-tax records are kept.''

''That would be great!'' said Dana. ''Here comes Sue,'' she added in a low voice. ''Don't say anything about it in front of her, because we're keeping it a secret until we know more.''

''How's Tyler?'' Sue asked as she walked up to them.

''I'll be all right. The turtle?'' Tyler called from behind the closed windows.

''What about the ridley?'' Dana said to Sue.

Sue was reaching into the back of her truck for the stretcher. ''I think the ridley's too far gone,'' she said sadly. ''Dr. Bucalo can check him out and make sure.''

CHAPTER FIVE

Tyler was a little uneasy on the way back to the Point in Sue's truck. His tongue and his lips hadn't stopped tingling, and he didn't know whether he was dizzy or just light-headed from sneezing so many times. Could he be getting worse?

When they got to the lighthouse, though, Aunt Lissa took a good look at him and said reassuringly, "You were sitting just a few feet from the bay for an hour or more, and, thanks to the waves and wind, you got a heavy dose of red tide." She went on, "Why don't you lie down for a while, breathe it out of your system, and you'll feel much better. But don't open your bedroom window, or you'll be right back where you started," she warned. Tyler's room in the lighthouse caught the wind off Badger Bay.

Tyler fell asleep for half an hour, with Jake keeping him company. When he woke up, his face was back to normal, and the sneezing had stopped. But he understood, just a little, about what red tide could do to the animals that swam through it.

Tyler was helping his aunt set the kitchen table for dinner when Dana came in from the stranding barn.

"The little ridley didn't make it," she reported sadly. "Dr. Bucalo did an autopsy, and his stomach was full of clams, which is the worst."

"Why?" Tyler asked.

"Clams eat by filtering microscopic food out of seawater, and that includes poisonous algae," Aunt Lissa said. "The algae don't bother the clams, but poison builds up in their bodies—"

"And the clams become totally poisonous themselves," Dana said.

"Even humans can die from eating a single clam affected by red tide," said Aunt Lissa.

"So that little ridley never had a chance," Tyler said.

"But the loggerhead that Jane and Sue brought in earlier is going to make it," Dana added. "Plus Lou Green just showed up with another ridley, and this one's in better shape than ours was."

"So how many turtles are in the stranding barn right now?" Tyler asked her.

"Two living ones," Dana said.

"Aunt Lissa, did either of us get any phone calls?" Tyler asked suddenly.

"Oh, yes," his aunt said, shaking her head. "It's been so hectic around here that I forgot all about it. Charlie Mote called before you got home."

''Am I supposed to call him back?'' said Tyler, wondering if Charlie had already found out about the old building on the inlet.

''Yes—when I asked if there was any message I could give you, he said, 'Just tell Tyler the news isn't great,' '' Aunt Lissa replied.

What could Charlie have meant? Tyler looked at Dana, who shrugged.

''I hope nothing's wrong at the Motes',,'' Aunt Lissa said.

''Uh-uh—Charlie likes sounding mysterious,'' Tyler told her, heading for the hall phone.

Charlie picked up his phone on the second ring.

''It's Tyler,'' Tyler said in a low voice, because he didn't want Aunt Lissa to overhear anything. ''What—''

''Granddad says the building belongs to an old lady named Mercer,'' Charlie told him. ''And he says she's the cheapest human around. She's never given away a dime in her entire life, which goes double for a building.''

''Bummer,'' Tyler murmured.

They *had* to have that building, not just for Aunt Lissa but for Project Neptune.

Dana and Jake had followed Tyler into the hall.

''What's Charlie saying?'' Dana whispered. Now Aunt Lissa was standing at the kitchen sink, washing lettuce.

''Tell you in a second,'' Tyler said. ''Charlie, do you

know where this old lady lives?'' he whispered into the phone.

''Yeah, Granddad says she has a big place in the city. But she has a house here, too, and she comes to Rockport most weekends,'' Charlie replied.

Weekends? It was Thursday already.

''Find out where her house is. We'll go over there first thing Saturday morning and talk to her,'' said Tyler. ''If we explain about Project Neptune, and having to turn away stranded animals . . .''

''Grandad doesn't think it'll make any difference,'' Charlie said doubtfully.

''We won't know if we don't try,'' Tyler said, staying hopeful. ''See you.''

''Later,'' said Charlie.

As soon as Tyler hung up, though, the phone rang again. He grabbed it and said, ''Yeah, Charlie?''

But he heard a girl's voice on the other end of the line. ''No, it's Stephanie. Stephanie Marin? Are you feeling okay, Tyler?''

''Hey, Stephanie,'' said Tyler. ''I'm fine. What's up?''

''I told Dana I'd find out about that building on Wood Duck Inlet from my mom,'' Stephanie said. ''And she knew which one right away. It belongs to somebody named Mary Mercer who owns a lot of property around Rockport, like most of the stores on Main Street.''

''Thanks, Stephanie,'' Tyler said.

After he repeated everything to Dana, she said,

"Great! Then there's absolutely no reason for Mary Mercer to hang onto that useless old building on the inlet."

"No reason at all," Tyler said.

Was Aunt Lissa's birthday gift in the bag?

At lunch the next day in the school cafeteria, the Mote twins explained how to get to Mary Mercer's house.

"We go up Roanoke, around the curve, and past the Elk Lodge," Carter said.

"A two-story blue house on the hill," said Charlie.

"I think I know the one you mean," Dana said slowly. "There's a tall iron fence around it?"

"Isn't that the place where we got chased by dogs one Halloween?" Kim said all of a sudden.

"When we were seven years old," Dana said, nodding. "They were big, hairy, and weird-looking. I used to have nightmares about them."

"We dropped our Halloween candy when we ran, and the dogs ate it," Kim said.

"Then a woman opened the front door and yelled at us," Dana remembered. "She said we'd be in very hot water if her dogs got sick."

"And that was Mary Mercer?" said Hallie. She added, "She has pets, which means she must like animals."

But Kim said, "Maybe this isn't such a good idea."

"Are *you* chickening out?" Hallie asked Dana.

When Dana didn't answer immediately, Tyler said firmly, ''Of course we're not.''

''This hotel's just about full,'' Aunt Lissa said woefully when the cousins walked through the side door of the barn that afternoon.

Tyler's aunt wasn't kidding. Every wire cage was occupied. Grayish-brown harbor seals dozed peacefully on their sides. Ellie the grey seal was sniffing the air, eager for dinner. A newly arrived harp seal huddled fearfully at the back of its cage, a sweep of black fur curving down its white sides like wings. Neptuners had brought in a couple of large, plastic dog carriers to accommodate the two baby seals finally well enough to leave Dr. Bucalo's clinic.

''All three turtle tanks in here are already taken,'' a Neptuner named Tom Kelly said as he edged past them with a bucket. ''And one of the exercise tanks has a new resident.''

''Who?'' Tyler said, walking to the row of fiberglass tanks in the middle of the barn.

He peered over the edge of the first one. Tyler had expected to see a seal gliding smoothly through the water. Instead . . . ''Whoa!'' he exclaimed.

An enormous turtle with a strange-looking, bumpy back was splayed out at the bottom of the tank. It raised its huge head to stare at Tyler. Then it hissed a loud warning.

''What is that thing?'' Tyler said to Dana. ''It's the size of a minivan!''

Dana checked out the turtle. ''It's a leatherback,'' she said. ''They're called that because they're the only sea turtles without hard shells.''

Tom Kelly joined them beside the tank. ''The grown-ups weigh around two thousand pounds. Luckily, this one's not an adult,'' he told Tyler. ''Still, it took six strong guys to get her in here.''

''What do they eat?'' Tyler asked, trying to imagine what it would take to fill up a leatherback weighing two thousand pounds.

''Jellyfish,'' Dana told him. ''Tons of them.''

''So this one ate lots of jellyfish polluted with red tide algae and ended up—'' Tyler began.

''Uh-uh. Leatherbacks are deepwater turtles, and red tide's a shallow-water problem. But they do have run-ins with boats and get tangled in fishnets. . . . See the back left flipper?'' Tom said.

Tyler nodded. A deep red groove ran across the flipper from one side to the other.

''Her flipper had been sawed almost in two by the time a fisherman found this young lady trailing a net near Perth Island,'' Tom said.

Carol Prentice stopped by to tell Tom: ''We put a pair ridleys in the tanks in the lighthouse, because it's warmer in there.'' Carol was Project Neptune's book-keeper when she wasn't helping out in the barn.

‘‘So there’s no room left for any more turtles?’’ Dana said to her.

‘‘Not unless we borrow your bathtubs,’’ Carol said, ‘‘which we may have to do.’’

‘‘The turtles need that building on the inlet!’’ Dana murmured to Tyler once Carol and Tom had walked away from them. ‘‘And Mom needs a fortieth birthday present. I can handle a visit to Mary Mercer on Saturday—don’t worry.’’

CHAPTER SIX

After breakfast the next morning, Dana and Tyler met Hallie and the Motes in front of Griffing Hardware. A few minutes later, Kim rode up on her bike.

"I didn't know you were coming with us," Dana said, really pleased.

"I decided *more* kids might make a bigger impression on Mary Mercer," Kim said. "Or at least on her dogs. Have you seen Cassie this morning?"

"Cassie?" Dana said, puzzled. "Why?"

"I ran into her at Main Street Sweets yesterday afternoon, and she asked what I was doing on Saturday. So I thought she might show up here," Kim said.

"Like Cassie cares about helping Project Neptune," Hallie said.

The group headed around the corner to Roanoke. It didn't take them long to reach the blue house on the hill. A tall wrought-iron fence framed an open lawn, just as Dana had remembered. Next to the heavy gate, a red-and-white sign warned: NO TRESPASSING.

"Really friendly," Hallie said.

"She'll probably have us arrested just for being on her property," said Kim.

"We'll leave our stuff out here," Tyler said, leaning his bike against the fence.

"Yeah, for a quick getaway," Kim said.

Tyler was already lifting the latch and pushing open the gate. He stepped onto the long sidewalk leading to the front door.

"Are you guys coming?" he said over his shoulder to the rest of them.

This is for Mom. And the turtles, Dana told herself. "You bet," she added out loud.

Dana took a deep breath and stepped through the gate. Hallie and the Motes followed her, with Kim at the end of the line.

"Big yard," Carter said.

"Great view!" said Hallie.

"That's Anchor Inlet, past the big pine tree," said Charlie.

Dana didn't take her eyes off the front door of the blue house, though. Her heart was starting to pound in her ears. She walked slower and slower.

Tyler marched straight up the front steps. He grabbed the brass door knocker and tapped on the door.

Dana paused on the top step, and the other kids gathered at the bottom.

"Maybe Ms. Mercer's in the city. Or sleeping," Kim said in a low voice. "Maybe we should go."

Tyler knocked again, louder this time. Almost immediately, Dana heard a dog bark. Then another. And another.

"They're still here," Kim said nervously from the sidewalk.

"But there are six of us this time," Hallie pointed out, "and we're big—not just two little kids trick-or-treating."

Suddenly the front door sprang open, and three large animals burst through it, barking loudly. They were so completely covered with long, ropy, white curls that it was hard to figure out their shapes. Only the tips of their noses showed through the mass of fur.

"These are commodores!" Hallie exclaimed over the racket.

"Komondors!" a voice corrected her sternly.

A tall, white-haired woman stepped out of the house. "They're a Hungarian breed. Down, Miklos! No, Bela! Quiet, Kartal!" she commanded.

She pushed the dogs back toward the open door, but they wriggled away from her. They danced around and barked even louder.

"What are you children doing here? Didn't you see the sign at the gate?" the woman asked sharply.

"Ms. Mercer?" said Tyler.

"Yes, and who are you?" Ms. Mercer said.

"I'm Tyler Chapin, and this is my cousin Dana,"

Tyler said. ''We wanted to talk to you about Project Neptune—''

''You're selling magazines or raffle tickets, and I'm not interested in buying any,'' Ms. Mercer said firmly. She was ready to go back inside the house with her Hungarian dogs.

''No, wait—we're not selling anything,'' Dana said quickly. She stepped up beside Tyler. ''Project Neptune rescues stranded seals and sea turtles. And we're running out of room for all of the animals we take in, especially now that there's a red tide.''

''And?'' said Ms. Mercer, peering at Dana closely. Dana hoped she wasn't remembering that Halloween evening six years ago. ''What does this project have to do with me?'' Ms. Mercer wanted to know.

''You own an old building on Wood Duck Inlet,'' Dana began.

''I do?'' Ms. Mercer said. Then she nodded. ''Oh, yes—I do,'' she agreed. ''The old boatyard.''

''Since no one has used it for years,'' Dana said, ''we wondered if you'd be willing to donate it to Project Neptune, to use as another stranding barn.''

Ms. Mercer stared at them in silence.

''The building's in okay shape,'' Hallie said from the bottom step. ''It's not like you'd have to do anything to it.''

''We could fix whatever needs to be fixed ourselves,'' Charlie said.

''It would solve a lot of our problems,'' Tyler said.

Ms. Mercer still hadn't said anything. Dana was beginning to wonder if she had understood what they were asking. But the white-haired woman suddenly exclaimed: "You want me to *give* you a *building?*"

"You're not using it, are you?" Hallie asked.

"That's neither here nor there," Ms. Mercer said, pulling the komondors toward the house again. "Red tides and turtles have nothing to do with me. Good day." As soon as she'd gotten the dogs safely inside, she slammed the door closed.

"She sounds like Cassie Parker," Hallie sniffed.

A few seconds later, the door opened a crack. "If you've been trespassing at Wood Duck Inlet," Ms. Mercer warned, "you're breaking the law, and you're risking legal action."

The door closed again, but the barking went on.

"What a sweetheart!" Hallie muttered.

"She's as cheap as Granddad said," Charlie added.

"We might as well go," said Carter.

"Before she turns the dogs loose," Kim agreed.

Tyler sneezed a few times as they headed down the walk toward their bikes. "Do you think there's any way we could change her mind?" he said to Dana.

"Not in this lifetime," Dana said, feeling miserable. "Now we only have a week to think of a gift for Mom. And what'll happen to the turtles?"

CHAPTER SEVEN

"We have turtles coming out of our ears," Mr. Garber said to Tyler and Dana when they got back to the Point later that morning.

Mr. Garber was the oldest Neptuner, and he'd found a green turtle washed ashore on the far side of Rockport. The green turtle, which was actually brownish, was resting comfortably in an old bathtub someone had set up outside the stranding barn.

Next to the bathtub, Donny Nolan had popped a small leatherback into a wading pool that belonged to his four-year-old niece.

And Walter McGrath had brought in a young loggerhead. It barely fit into the well of a wheelbarrow.

Tyler's uncle and aunt were taking stock of their containers.

"Goldings is sending us two more tanks," Aunt Lissa murmured as she checked a list. "And we've already used everything else we've got except a water-garden liner from Lerner's Landscaping.''

''I talked to the people at Cape Mayo,'' Uncle Joe said to Tyler and Dana. ''Red tide is starting up there, too, so they don't expect to have much extra room.''

''How long will it take the turtles to get over their symptoms?'' Tyler asked his uncle.

He was remembering how fast he'd recovered from his own exposure to the poisons in the air. If the same was true of turtles, some of the tanks might be free again soon.

''If a turtle doesn't die right away because it can't breathe, the effects of the algae usually fade after a few days,'' Uncle Joe said. ''Sometimes we can force activated charcoal mixed with water down their throats and neutralize the poison more quickly.''

''But we can't release the turtles even if they're well, not as long as the poisonous algae are multiplying in the bay and in the inlets,'' Aunt Lissa pointed out.

''We'd better pray for a cold snap,'' said Mr. Garber.

Tyler and Dana worked in the stranding barn for a couple of hours. They helped Sue Larkin and Bonnie Bishop shift seals in and out of the two free exercise tanks so that their cages could be cleaned. Each time a seal finished swimming, the tank had to be drained, disinfected with bleach, and refilled before the next seal could dive in. That way, the animals wouldn't pass any germs around.

The kids grabbed a quick lunch of sandwiches and chips at the lighthouse, along with Tim Gilmore, Lou Green, and a few more hungry Neptuners. Tyler was glad to have the company, because he didn't really feel like rehashing the visit to Ms. Mercer's with Dana. What was there to say?

But Tyler couldn't stop worrying about the turtles. Not to mention Aunt Lissa's birthday present!

After they'd washed dishes, he and Dana were heading out to the stranding barn again when they noticed a black car rolling up the gravel road.

''Somebody's bringing us another sick sea turtle,'' Dana said with a groan.

But Tyler took a closer look at the car and said, ''Dana, isn't that Cassie's mom?''

''Mrs. Parker?'' Dana said, peering at the car herself. ''It *is*. Why is she here?'' Dana added, ''I think Cassie's sitting in the backseat.''

''It looks like she's doing aerobics!'' Tyler said, because Cassie's arms seemed to be flying up and down, up and down. . . .

Then Mrs. Parker spotted Tyler and Dana. She waved and stepped on the gas pedal.

When the car stopped beside them with a crunching of gravel, Mrs. Parker practically shouted, ''Thank goodness!''

''Is anything wrong?'' Dana said to her.

''Oh, Dana, am I glad to see you!'' Cassie called from the backseat.

Tyler peered through thc closed window. Cassie was wrestling with something that was totally covered with a pink blanket.

"What have you got under there?" Tyler asked her through the glass. Whatever it was, it was much too lively for a turtle and too small to be a seal.

"It's an enormous bird!" Cassie said, as huge wings flailed under the blanket. "I think he must have eaten some dead fish. I was walking near the inlet, and suddenly I saw him staggering around, trying to fly. But he couldn't get off the ground. So I ran to the house for a blanket to throw over him, like Mr. Foley told us to—"

"I'll get Mom!" Dana said. She raced toward the stranding barn.

"Don't let that thing scratch you again, Cassie!" Mrs. Parker warned nervously, turning to peek into the backseat at her daughter. "You be careful, too, Tyler," she added.

Tyler was opening the car door as quietly as he could. He slid slowly onto the backseat himself.

Cassie was hugging the bird's wings against its sides. Tyler noticed the tops of her fingers were bleeding, as though they'd been raked by claws. Suddenly the bird screeched a couple of times and struggled so furiously that it managed to poke its head out from under the folds of the blanket.

Tyler found himself gazing into a fierce, golden eye!

The eye stared out of a wide band of dark-brown

feathers, below a white crest. Tyler saw the top of a curved yellow beak . . .

Then Cassie yelled, "Cover him up!"

Tyler grabbed an edge of the blanket and dropped it over the bird's head.

"That's no seagull," he said.

"No kidding!" Cassie said, breathless from her efforts. "I think it must be some kind of eagle."

The big bird was still fighting to get away from her. And then, all at once, it stopped. It slumped to one side, motionless.

"Is he dead?" Cassie asked, her voice shaky.

Dana was back with Aunt Lissa. Tyler's aunt opened the car door and reached across Cassie for the blanket-covered bird.

"No, he's not dead," Aunt Lissa said, hugging the bundle to her chest with both arms and straightening up. "I can feel his heart beating. I'll take him right in to Dr. Bucalo."

She hurried toward the clinic just beyond the stranding barn, with Dana following.

"Thank you so much," Mrs. Parker called after them. "And that's that. Cassie, why don't you get into the front seat?" she went on as Tyler climbed out of the car. "We're late already, and—"

"No, I want to stay here until I know if the bird's going to be okay," Cassie said, sliding out of the backseat and standing next to Tyler.

''But you'll miss your piano lesson,'' said Mrs. Parker.

''Mom!'' Cassie said sharply. ''I'm not leaving until I find out what kind of bird it is, at least!''

''Uncle Joe or Aunt Lissa can drive Cassie home, Mrs. Parker,'' Tyler said quickly.

''Well . . . all right,'' said Mrs. Parker. Frowning, she started her car. ''We're having guests for dinner, Cassie,'' Mrs. Parker said. ''I'll expect you by five.''

''Okay, okay,'' Cassie muttered. ''Can we see the bird?'' she asked Tyler after her mother drove away.

''Let's go to the clinic,'' Tyler said.

Dana met them halfway. ''Dr. Bucalo's working with the osprey right now,'' Dana said to Cassie. ''He hopes it's going to make it.''

''An osprey?'' Cassie said.

''They're also called fish hawks,'' Dana told her.

''Which is practically an eagle,'' Cassie said to Tyler.

''They nest along the coast. They've been in trouble for years, because of insecticides and water pollution,'' Dana said. ''This one's wearing a tag, which probably means a lot of people are tracking his migration route back and forth from South America.''

''I felt so sorry for him,'' Cassie said in a low voice. ''He was so beautiful. And so scared.''

''You did a really good thing, bringing him to the Point, Cassie,'' Dana said. ''You saved his life.''

''Cassie needs a ride home, Dana,'' Tyler said.

''Not just yet,'' Cassie said. ''What have you got in those tubs?'' she asked, pointing toward the odd collection of containers lined up outside the stranding barn.

''Different kinds of sea turtles,'' Dana told her.

''Sea turtles?'' said Cassie.

Tyler expected her to add, ''Yuck!'' But she didn't.

Cassie said, ''Can I take a look?''

CHAPTER EIGHT

It was definitely a day of ups and downs.

First Dana and Tyler had had their run-in with Ms. Mercer about the birthday building. They'd ridden home completely discouraged, only to find more sea turtles arriving at the Point, with fewer and fewer places to put them.

But when everything seemed to be totally dismal, Cassie Parker had shown up at Project Neptune with an osprey *she*'d rescued. Who could ever have predicted that?

And after Cassie had turned the osprey over to Dana's mom, she actually asked if she could take a look at the sea turtles before she left for home.

"They're not all so hideous," Cassie said, gazing at the young leatherback in the wading pool outside the barn. "Actually, this one's kind of cute."

"Want to see what he'll be like when he grows up?" Tyler said to her. He grinned at Dana.

But even the huge leatherback in the stranding barn didn't discourage Cassie.

"Wow—it's like *Jurassic Park!*" she said, as the huge turtle hissed at them.

"Turtles were around *before* the dinosaurs," Dana told her. "They've been on earth for one hundred and fifty million years."

"It's really sad to think they could become extinct after all that time," said Cassie. "And it's just because of us?"

She's beginning to get it, Dana told herself. *Cassie might make a Neptuner after all.*

Cassie had definitely gotten attached to the osprey. "Can I visit him tomorrow?" she asked Dana.

"Probably," Dana said. "Mom was talking about having Tim Gilmore and Lou Green build a big outdoor cage for him to recuperate in."

"Great!" Cassie said. "I'll ride my bike over in the morning."

"Hey, Cassie—it's almost four-thirty," Tyler said, checking his watch. "Your dinner?" he reminded her.

"I guess I'd better go," Cassie said with a sigh.

Dana's mom and dad were both busy helping Dr. Bucalo in the clinic. But Sue Larkin said, "I'll be glad to drive you home, Cassie. I'm on my way into town to buy some supplies, so I'll drop you off."

"Why don't you guys come, too?" Cassie said to Tyler and Dana. "I can show you where I found the osprey. And since they're migrating right now, another might have . . ."

She didn't finish her sentence, but Dana thought Cassie might be afraid that there were more sick birds on her beach.

"Sure, we'll ride in with you," Dana said, adding, "if that's okay, Sue?"

Sue nodded. "You can help me shop."

The four of them squeezed into the front of Sue's truck. She made sure they kept the windows rolled up on the way to town because of Tyler's problems with the wind off the bay.

When they got to the Parkers' house, Sue waited in the truck while Dana and Tyler followed Cassie across the lawn and down to Anchor Inlet. Tall reeds and marsh grass bordered a narrow beach strewn with dead fish.

"The osprey was flopping around over there," Cassie said, pointing to a big piece of driftwood about fifty feet away from them. "I didn't notice him at first because I was staring at those brownish patches in the water—"

"Red tide," Dana said. And Tyler sneezed.

"You shouldn't even be here," Dana said to Tyler.

"I'll go back to the truck in a second," Tyler said, sneezing again.

"Then I heard this thumping noise," Cassie went on. "It was the osprey's wings hitting that driftwood while he tried to take off. But he was too weak to fly."

As the three of them stared up the beach toward the

driftwood, Dana noticed a large, whitish mound not far beyond it. It could have been dirty rags or wet paper or . . .

"What is that?" Tyler asked, spotting it, too.

"Some garbage that washed ashore?" Cassie guessed.

"Uh-uh—I think it moved!" Dana exclaimed suddenly. "Tyler, you should get away from the water," she warned her cousin again, before she sprinted up the beach.

As Dana got nearer, the mound stopped looking like a pile of wet paper or rags, and started looking more a fishnet. Or ropes. Or . . .

Dana gasped. "Tyler, it's a komondor!" she yelled over her shoulder. "Get Sue!"

"A commodore?" said Cassie, catching up with Dana.

"A dog!" Dana said.

She flung herself down next to the big white animal. Maybe he had moved before, but now he was motionless, collapsed on his stomach with his head tilted to one side. A broken clamshell lay on the sand not six inches from his nose.

"Is he alive?" Cassie asked softly.

Dana lay her head on the dog's side. "I don't think he's breathing," she said.

Dana had once watched her mom and Dr. Bucalo give artificial respiration to a hooded seal. She tried frantically to remember what they'd done.

Get a grip! she told herself. *First you feel for a pulse.*

Dana slid her hand down to where the inside of the dog's back leg met his body. *He's so hairy, it's hard to feel anything,* she thought. But all at once her fingers found his pulse, pounding like a snare drum. The dog's heart was racing, desperate for oxygen.

"Cassie, pull all four of his legs straight out to the left," Dana said. "Hurry."

"He's so *heavy!*" Cassie said. But she managed to straighten out each of the dog's legs so that he was lying flat on his right side.

Dana scrambled up to the dog's head and opened his mouth, to make sure nothing was blocking his throat. Aside from a few bits of clamshell stuck in his teeth, his mouth looked okay.

Then Dana scooted around to kneel next to the dog's spine. She placed the heels of both hands on the dog's rib cage, just behind his left front elbow, and she pushed down, hard. She let up, then pressed again, fast, six times in a row.

Dana stopped pressing for a full five seconds, to give the dog's chest a chance to expand, and hopefully pull in some air. "One . . . two . . . three . . . four . . . five," she counted out loud. Then Dana started pressing down again: "One, up, two, up, three, up, four, up, five, up, six. Rest. One . . . two . . . three . . . four . . . five."

"I think I saw his side move," Cassie whispered. "Is he breathing yet?"

"He just has to be," Dana said. She continued to press and rest, press and rest.

By the time Sue and Tyler ran up the beach with a tarp from Sue's truck, Dana was worn out.

"Good work!" Sue said to Dana as she checked out the dog. "He's breathing a little on his own. Let's roll him over onto this." Sue laid the tarp out on the sand beside the komondor. Pulling and pushing, the four of them slid the limp animal onto it.

Then Sue, Dana, Tyler, and Cassie each grabbed a corner of the tarp and headed down the beach with the dog, toward the Parkers' yard.

"We're pretty sure we know who he belongs to," Dana said to Sue as they struggled along. "Ms. Mercer—she has a house on the inlet, too."

"Shouldn't we call her?" Cassie asked.

"No time—we'll drive him straight to the Point," said Sue. "Dr. Bucalo knows more about treating red-tide poisoning than anybody in this part of the state."

"*If* he makes it," Dana said uneasily. The dog's head lolled from side to side with every step they took.

"Has he stopped breathing again?" asked Tyler.

"Hold on," Sue said. "Let me try something."

As soon as they lowered the tarp to the sand, Sue opened the dog's mouth to pull his tongue forward. Then she closed his mouth again and held his lips tightly together with her hand.

Sue put her mouth right over the dog's nose and blew hard for a few seconds, forcing air into his nostrils.

''Ick!'' Cassie murmured.

But the dog's side moved as his lungs expanded.

''Cool,'' said Tyler.

And Dana said, ''Wow!''

Sue raised her head briefly. Then she blew into the dog's nose again. She kept it up for a few minutes, until the dog seemed to have started breathing on his own.

''Let's get him to the truck as fast as we can!'' Sue said.

As they were crossing the Parkers' yard with the dog on the tarp, Mrs. Parker called out a window: ''Cassie, the Werners will be arriving soon. Please come in and get ready for dinner!''

''I need to be *here* right now,'' Cassie said.

''Cassie!'' said Mrs. Parker.

''We're putting a very sick dog in the truck!'' Cassie said impatiently.

Sue lowered the tailgate with one hand. She and Tyler climbed into the bed of the truck, lifting up their end of the tarp and walking backward with it.

''Okay . . . set him down gently,'' Sue said to everybody.

Soon the komondor was lying flat on his side in the truck. His breathing was shallow and labored.

''I'm afraid he won't make it to the Point without some help,'' Sue said, watching the dog uneasily. ''Do you think your mother or dad might drive us, so I could stay in the back of the truck with him?'' she asked Cassie.

Cassie shook her head. "Not with the Werners coming to dinner," she said. "Mr. Werner is my dad's boss."

"I'll ride with the dog," Dana said to Sue. "I'll do what you were doing."

"We'll take turns," said Tyler, coughing and clearing his throat.

"No way," Sue said to him. "You're sitting inside, and we don't have time for arguments."

"I'll ride in the back with Dana!" Cassie said suddenly.

"But your mom—" Dana began.

Cassie had already climbed into the back of the truck. She sat down beside the dog.

Sue had to drive slowly, because she didn't want the girls, or the sick dog, to get bounced around. Dana breathed for the komondor for ten minutes or so. Then Cassie took a deep breath . . . and put her mouth right over the dog's nose. And she kept it up until they turned onto the gravel road at the Point.

"We made it!" Dana said as they rolled toward the clinic.

"I'll bet my mother's going to ground me for weeks," Cassie said, sitting up. "But I don't care—the dog's still breathing!"

Tyler ran into the stranding barn as soon as Sue stopped the truck. Dana's mom and dad and Brian Wilson rushed back out with him. Along with Sue, they carried the dog into the clinic.

“Should we call that Mercer person?” Tyler said to Dana and Cassie.

“I’d want to know right away if somebody found Jake,” Dana said.

“She’s probably not even listed,” said Tyler as they headed for the lighthouse.

But Dana found the number in the Rockport directory. “Here it is—Mary Mercer on Roanoke. You call her, Tyler,” she said, showing him the number.

As soon as he’d finished dialing on the hall phone, though, he handed the receiver to Dana.

“Thanks a lot!” she said, and listened to the rings. One, two . . .

“Hello?” a sharp voice said on the other end of the line.

“Ms. Mercer?” Dana said.

“Who is this?” said Ms. Mercer.

“Dana Chapin. I met you this morning,” Dana said.

“And I thought I made it clear that—” Ms. Mercer began.

But Dana interrupted her. “We found one of your dogs, Ms. Mercer,” she said.

“You *what?*” Ms. Mercer said. She clunked the phone down and immediately started calling out, “Miklos! Bela! Kartal!”

Then Dana heard her say, “Good boy, Kartal. You are, too, Miklos.” Then she said, “But where is Bela?”

Footsteps, and Ms. Mercer yelling, “Bela! Bela?”

She hurried back to the phone. "Do you have Bela?! Just where are you?"

"The lighthouse at Parsons Point," Dana said. "It's on Harbor Lane, about five miles from—"

"I know!" Ms. Mercer slammed the phone down.

"That was weird," Dana said, hanging up the hall phone.

"Is she coming?" Cassie asked.

"I guess so," Dana said. "She didn't ask why we had the dog, or if the dog was all right, or anything."

CHAPTER NINE

Ms. Mercer must have jumped in her car the instant she hung up the phone and driven full speed up Harbor Lane. Tyler barely had time to open a soda before he heard a car pulling up outside the lighthouse.

The girls were sitting at the kitchen table, talking and patting Jake.

''I think she's here,'' Tyler told them.

''Ms. Mercer? How could she be?'' Dana said, scooting her chair back.

Two seconds later, there was a loud knock at the back door.

When Tyler opened it, Ms. Mercer was standing there. She peered past Tyler into the kitchen and gazed suspiciously at Dana and Cassie and at Jake, who was under the table, wagging his tail.

Then Ms. Mercer demanded: ''Well, where is he? What have you done with my Bela?''

Dana tried to explain: "We brought him to the clinic—"

At the same time, Cassie said, "Your dog ate a bad clam from the inlet and—"

"He wasn't breathing," Tyler said.

But Ms. Mercer wasn't listening to any of them. She was too angry.

"Maybe you see this as a harmless prank. But komondors are very high-strung," she stormed. "What if you've caused him permanent emotional damage?" She added, "You kidnapped my dog, and I'm not willing to let this go unpunished!"

"Excuse me! Who are *you?* And just what do you mean by 'kidnapped'?" Aunt Lissa was marching up the back steps.

Ms. Mercer whirled around to ask her, "Are you in charge of these . . . these *children?*"

"You owe these *children* an apology!" Aunt Lissa said fiercely. "This is my daughter, my nephew, and a friend of theirs. And if your dog lives, it'll be due almost entirely to their efforts!"

"If my dog *lives?*" Ms. Mercer squeaked, finally paying attention. "What's happened to him? Where is he? Please take me to him!"

"Come with me," Aunt Lissa said. She started down the steps again, with Ms. Mercer following her. "Cassie, I'll be back to take you home," she added.

"Wow," Tyler said, as he, Dana, and Cassie watched

them hurrying toward the clinic. ''Aunt Lissa hardly ever gets mad. But when she does . . . look out!''

''What a horrible old lady!'' Cassie said about Ms. Mercer, making a face.

''But I hope Bela is okay,'' Dana said. ''Those dogs are probably the only things Ms. Mercer cares about.''

When Aunt Lissa came back to the lighthouse a few minutes later, she was alone.

''Ms. Mercer will stay at the clinic for a while,'' Aunt Lissa said, then paused for a moment before continuing. ''I'm sure the only reason she was unpleasant to you was because she was so upset. Okay?''

Dana nodded.

Tyler said, ''Sure, Aunt Lissa.'' Privately he thought, *Ms. Mercer was unpleasant because that's how she is.* And he was pretty certain that Dana agreed with him.

''Cassie, are you ready to go?'' Aunt Lissa asked, taking their truck keys off the kitchen counter.

''I guess I'd better be,'' Cassie said reluctantly. ''But I'll see you tomorrow,'' she told Dana and Tyler. ''And my osprey. If I'm not grounded.''

''Will you two give Bonnie and Claude their dinner, please?'' Aunt Lissa said as she and Cassie left the lighthouse.

Tyler and Dana collected eight packages of frozen herring from the food-prep shed and carried them over to the outdoor tank. Bonnie and Claude zoomed up to the edge and clicked impatiently while Tyler tore open the first package.

He was tossing a fish to Claude when Dana said, ''Look, Tyler—Ms. Mercer's leaving.''

Tyler turned around in time to see her climb into her long blue car. He and Dana watched Ms. Mercer back away from the lighthouse and steer the car onto the gravel road.

As she rolled slowly past them, her head drooped, and Dana said, ''She's crying.''

Ms. Mercer didn't glance in their direction. Staring straight ahead, she drove to Harbor Lane and turned toward Rockport.

''Do you think her dog . . . died?'' Tyler asked.

He remembered how full of energy the komondors had been just hours before.

''As soon as we finish feeding these guys, let's go find out,'' Dana said, tearing open another package of fish.

When they walked into the clinic, the first thing they saw was the osprey. The bird was still a little wobbly, but he was standing up, examining them from inside a wire cage in a corner of the front room.

''He is one tough-looking dude,'' Tyler murmured admiringly.

The osprey was at least two feet tall, and mostly white, with dark-brown feathers on his back and upper wings, and brown eyestripes.

''Major claws,'' Tyler added, noticing the bird's feet. ''And huge wings.''

''Ospreys have a six-foot wingspan,'' Dana whispered. "They can fly eighty miles an hour when they're going after a fish."

Suddenly the osprey squawked loudly and ruffled his feathers. The door to the examining room swung open, and Dr. Bucalo and Sue Larkin stepped through it.

"At least one patient is doing well," Dr. Bucalo said in a low voice, glancing at the osprey.

"What about the komondor?" Tyler asked him.

"We forced some activated charcoal down his throat to counteract the poison. And he's breathing on his own," Dr. Bucalo said. "If he makes it through the night, he'll be on his way to a complete recovery."

"How was Ms. Mercer?" Dana wanted to know.

"Not an easy lady," said Sue.

"I think she was angry with herself for not keeping her dog in the house, away from the red tide," said Dr. Bucalo.

"The turtles need us," Sue said then, reaching for the outer door.

"We tried to warn Ms. Mercer about the red tide," Dana said to Tyler as they walked back to the lighthouse.

"And she was so sure it had nothing to do with her," said Tyler.

It wasn't exactly an "I told you so"—Tyler didn't want the komondor to die. But he knew that anything happening to the environment eventually affected *everything* in the environment. And Ms. Mercer had found that out the hard way.

* * *

After dinner that night, Tyler and Dana were watching a movie on TV when Uncle Joe sneaked into the living room. ''What about your mom?'' he asked Dana in a whisper. ''Have you and Tyler had any ideas about her party?''

The cousins shook their heads. Their best birthday idea was down the tubes.

''Have you thought of anything, Dad?'' Dana asked him.

''We've been so busy with turtles that I haven't had time to think at all,'' Uncle Joe admitted. ''Come on, guys, we've only got a week left.''

Tyler woke up really early the next morning. When he slipped out of the house, he saw Dr. Bucalo's car parked outside the clinic. The veterinarian had probably slept there all night, to keep an eye on the komondor.

Tyler headed for the line of rocks edging Badger Bay. Even in the low light of dawn, he could see large splotches of reddish-brown algae spread across the blue-green water. And he sneezed twice.

I'm like an automatic red-tide alarm, Tyler said to himself, sneezing again.

He left the bay shore to take a look at the pilot whales. When he was halfway to the outdoor tank, a car turned onto the Point. Tyler stopped for a second to see which Neptuner was arriving so early.

But it wasn't a Neptuner at all. It was Ms. Mercer,

speeding up the gravel road. She looked over at Tyler, but she didn't slow down. She screeched to a stop beside the clinic, jumped out of her car, and hurried inside.

Dana, barely awake, wandered out of the lighthouse to where Tyler was standing. ''Maybe Dr. Bucalo phoned her to come,'' she said to him, looking at Ms. Mercer's car outside the clinic.

''Maybe the dog died after all,'' Tyler said.

''Poor Bela,'' Dana said. ''And poor Ms. Mercer,'' she added.

They watched Bonnie and Claude chase each other around the tank for a while. Then they headed toward the stranding barn. That's when they saw the long blue car rolling toward them, down the gravel road.

''She's leaving already,'' Tyler said to Dana.

''So we can go to the clinic and find out about her dog,'' Dana suggested.

But the car braked to a stop not twenty feet away from them. Ms. Mercer opened her door and got out. She had a strange expression on her face.

''Uh-oh,'' Dana said under her breath.

''Now what?'' said Tyler, fully expecting Ms. Mercer to start yelling at them again.

But she totally surprised them both. Ms. Mercer squared her shoulders and strode straight up to them. ''It seems I jumped to conclusions,'' she said. ''You saved my dog's life, and I'll always be grateful.''

''He's going to be okay?'' said Tyler.

"Bela is still weak, but Dr. Bucalo thinks I'll be able to take him home in a day or two," said Ms. Mercer.

"We're glad," Dana said.

Ms. Mercer stared down at the ground, and Tyler thought that was the end of their conversation. But suddenly she raised her head and continued: "I'm beginning to understand just how important an organization like Project Neptune can be."

Tyler and Dana glanced at each other.

"I'd like to speak to your parents about the boatyard on Wood Duck—" Ms. Mercer began.

"Oh, please don't," Dana interrupted. "If there's even a chance you might want to donate—"

"It's Aunt Lissa's birthday next week," Tyler explained, "and there's nothing she'd like more than—"

"Here comes Mom!" Dana hissed.

Aunt Lissa was hurrying down the steps of the lighthouse. She probably figured they needed protection from Ms. Mercer.

"Why don't you meet me at the inlet this afternoon," Ms. Mercer said quickly, "around four o'clock. And we'll talk about it."

"Thanks!" Dana murmured.

Ms. Mercer was getting back into her car when Aunt Lissa reached them.

"Good morning, Mrs. Chapin," Ms. Mercer said firmly before she drove away.

"Was she giving you a hard time?" Aunt Lissa asked Tyler and Dana.

''No, actually, she was apologizing for yelling at us,'' Tyler said.

Aunt Lissa nodded approvingly. ''As she should!'' she said.

CHAPTER TEN

Hallie Wade and the Mote twins showed up at the stranding barn a little later that morning. Dana and Tyler repeated the whole conversation with Ms. Mercer for them. Dana phoned Kim and told her. And Cassie Parker heard about it all when she arrived for a visit to the osprey.

So when Dana and Tyler biked to Wood Duck Inlet that afternoon, five kids were already waiting for them at the old boatyard.

''What time is it?'' Cassie asked as the cousins jumped off their bikes. ''I think my watch is slow.''

Dana checked her own watch: ''Three-fifty,'' she said.

''Do you think she's actually coming?'' Kim asked suspiciously, remembering how unpleasant Ms. Mercer had been just the day before.

''She said she would,'' was all Dana could reply.

"And you really believe she's going to give you this place?" said Cassie.

"She didn't say that, exactly. But I hope so," said Dana.

"Let's climb through the window again and look around," Charlie suggested. "We can start figuring out what needs to be done."

"Uh-uh," said Dana. "You know how Ms. Mercer feels about trespassing. If she finds us in the building, it could wreck everything!"

"So what are we supposed to do?" Hallie Wade said crossly.

"Sit here and wait," said Tyler.

Carter sketched in his notebook. Hallie and Charlie wandered toward the inlet. The rest of them sat down on tree stumps and waited. Tyler sneezed a few times.

Dana asked herself over and over again: *Has Ms. Mercer changed her mind?*

Finally, at about four-fifteen, she heard someone calling from beyond the pine thicket. "Hello-o-o?"

"Hello!" Tyler shouted.

"Is that her?" Kim said nervously.

"We're here!" Dana called back.

A minute or two later, Ms. Mercer walked purposefully up the dirt trail.

The sight of so many kids hanging around slowed her down a little. But then Ms. Mercer said, "I'm late because I wanted to see my lawyer first."

"I knew it. This was a trick, and now she's going to

put us in jail for being on her property!'' Kim whispered.

Carter looked uneasy, and Cassie muttered, ''We'll see about that—my aunt's a lawyer!''

''Come on, guys—let's hear what she has to say first,'' Dana said a low voice.

Ms. Mercer was sizing up the building. ''I haven't been here in years,'' she said. ''It's going to rack and ruin.''

''It's not that bad,'' Tyler said. ''Some of the windows are broken. But it's dry in—''

Dana nudged him to be quiet.

''I remember hearing about a brush fire,'' Ms. Mercer said, noticing the charred stumps. She reached into the top pocket of her jacket and pulled out a heavy key. ''We'd better take a look inside,'' she said.

The lock on the front doors was rusty and too stiff for Ms. Mercer to turn herself. But Carter managed to jiggle the key around until it worked. Then he and Tyler pulled hard on the doors, and they creaked open.

''Quite a large space,'' Ms. Mercer said, glancing around the big room.

''Large enough for lots of turtle tanks,'' Dana said.

''And some seals,'' said Tyler. ''Even a baby dolphin.''

''I think that wide door at the back faces Wood Duck Inlet,'' Ms. Mercer said. ''My father worked here when he was a boy,'' she added.

''Your dad fixed boats?'' Carter said, interested.

''Until he opened his own business,'' Ms. Mercer said. ''He built Halsted's Wharf, and named it for his mother's family.''

Then she looked straight at Dana and Tyler. ''Do you really think this place might be useful to Project Neptune? How would you get the animals in here? It would be very expensive to build a road,'' Ms. Mercer pointed out.

''We've thought about that,'' Dana said quickly. ''We could . . .''

That's when Hallie and Charlie edged through the front doors. Their jeans were soaking wet past the knees. They were carrying something heavy, slung between them in Hallie's yellow sweatshirt.

''We found a turtle floating in the inlet!'' Charlie puffed.

''Another Kemp's ridley,'' Hallie added, out of breath. ''How many does this make?''

And Ms. Mercer finished Dana's sentence. ''You could bring the animals up the inlet,'' she said.

''That's right,'' Dana said, before she and Tyler and the others ran to help Hallie and Charlie lower the turtle to the floor of the building. It just lay there, its flippers motionless.

''This guy doesn't look too good,'' Hallie murmured, kneeling down next to the ridley.

''We should get him to the Point as fast as we can,'' Dana said.

''On our bikes?'' Cassie said doubtfully.

''My car's parked near the curve at the end of Main Street,'' said Ms. Mercer. ''I'll drive you, if you can carry the turtle out of here.''

''Sure, we can do that,'' Tyler said.

''What about the building, Ms. Mercer?'' Dana asked.

They couldn't let it drop now, because they might never have another chance at it.

''Oh, yes—the building,'' Ms. Mercer repeated.

Everyone was listening, waiting to hear what she had to say.

Ms. Mercer reached into a side pocket of her jacket and pulled out some folded sheets of paper.

''These are for you,'' she said to Dana. ''I've signed them, and when you're ready to tell your parents about your plans for this building, they can sign them, too.''

Tyler looked at the papers over Dana's shoulder.

''They're three copies of an agreement,'' said Ms. Mercer, ''giving this building and all the land around it to Project Neptune.''

''Just like that?'' said Hallie from her place on the floor.

''Just like that,'' said Ms. Mercer. She handed Dana the heavy key to the front doors.

''Wow—thank you so much!'' Dana said breathlessly. She hugged Ms. Mercer, hard, without even thinking.

''It's . . . it's just good business,'' Ms. Mercer said briskly. ''It's a tax write-off for me.''

But Tyler said, ''It's a lot more than that.

And Dana thought Ms. Mercer looked almost pleased.

CHAPTER ELEVEN

At dinner that night, Aunt Lissa studied Tyler and Dana across the kitchen table and said, "You two seem excited about something."

"What's up?" asked Uncle Joe.

"Absolutely nothing, Dad," Dana said quickly.

"Just glad tomorrow's Monday," Tyler added.

Dana raised her eyebrows at him, and he shrugged. *Okay, that sounded dumb, but it's not so easy making up stuff on the spur of the moment,* Tyler thought.

"How are we ever going to keep this a secret for six days?" he whispered to Dana while they were clearing the dishes.

"Yeah, sometimes Mom has a way of reading our minds," Dana whispered back. "But at least it'll give us some time to fix the boatyard up."

They waited until Uncle Joe and Aunt Lissa went out to the stranding barn again. Then they grabbed the phone in the hall and called Tim Gilmore.

Besides being a long-time Neptuner, Tim was the manager at Ace Lumber, and they hoped he'd be able to help them with some quick repairs.

"Mary Mercer gave you a *building* for Project Neptune?" Tim said. "Amazing!"

"We want to surprise Mom on her birthday," Dana said, "which means we can't tell Dad about it, either. He'll forget that it's a secret."

"It'd be great if we could have Aunt Lissa's party there next Saturday," Tyler said into the phone.

"Tomorrow's my day off," Tim told them. "What do we need to do right away?"

"The roof leaks, and a lot of the windows are broken," Tyler told him.

"Maybe somebody could take a look at the wiring," Dana said.

"We could start painting inside," said Tyler.

"I'll line up Lou Green. He's a great carpenter and good with repairs. Walter and I can plaster and paint," Tim said. "So can Jane Hodges. If we don't want Lissa and Joe to catch on, though, we'll have to work around our regular hours at the Point. How do we get into the building?"

"Ms. Mercer gave us the key to the front doors," Dana said.

"I'll meet you in the middle school parking lot tomorrow morning to pick it up," Tim said. "Around eight o'clock, okay?"

"Thanks, Tim!" said Dana.

Before he hung up, Tim added, ''Your folks are going to be blown away, and so are all the Neptuners. It couldn't have come at a better time, either. We don't have an inch of space left at the stranding barn.''

The next morning, Tyler and Dana told Aunt Lissa and Uncle Joe that they'd be riding their bikes to school all that week.

''We have science reports to research at the public library, so we can't take the bus home in the afternoons,'' Dana said to her parents as she zipped up her backpack.

''I have a feeling this is going to get pretty complicated,'' she murmured to Tyler as they hurried down the back steps. ''I hate lying.''

They coasted up to Rockport Middle School just as Tim drove the Ace truck into the parking lot.

''Yo, Tim!'' said Tyler.

''This is the key to the boatyard,'' Dana said, handing it to him.

''I'll start hauling in supplies. What color do we want to paint the inside?'' Tim asked them.

''Light green?'' said Dana.

''Badger Bay blue?'' said Tyler.

''Anything but red-tide brown,'' Dana said.

''We'll start with a thick coat of white and go from there,'' Tim said. ''See you this afternoon,'' he added before he drove away.

During lunch, everybody at their table in the cafeteria tried to come up with a name for the new place.

Hallie said, "Ridley Refuge."

"We rescue lots of turtles that aren't ridleys," Kim pointed out.

"Sea Turtle Sanctuary," Dana suggested.

"That's okay," Cassie said, "but it's long. What about Neptune's Retreat?"

" 'Retreat' sounds like we're giving up," said Tyler.

"Neptune II?" said Charlie.

His brother shook his head, and Hallie said, "That's a good name for a dance club."

"Neptune's Annex?" said Tyler.

"I kind of like that," Hallie said after thinking about it for a couple of seconds.

"I do, too," said Kim.

"Not bad," said Dana. "The Annex," she added, trying it out.

"I'll start painting a sign," Carter said.

After school that day, Tyler, Dana, Charlie, and Hallie rode over to the Annex.

The Ace Lumber truck was parked near the curve at the end of Main Street. So was Lou's truck and Jane Hodges's Jeep. And before the group could see the Annex through the pines, they could hear hammering and the buzz of a battery-powered drill.

Lou waved to them from the roof. He'd pulled off a

lot of the damaged shingles. Now he was laying down new ones.

The kids dumped their bikes and hurried inside the old building.

"Wow!" said Tyler.

"I can't believe how much you guys have gotten done already!" Dana added.

Two of the inside walls had been patched and plastered, and Tim and Jane were working on a third. The glass in some of the windows had been replaced, too.

"What can we do?" Hallie asked.

"Grab some brooms," Jane said, waving at half a dozen brand-new ones leaning against a wall. "There are cobwebs in here older than you are."

The kids swept out dry leaves, dead bugs, cobwebs, and rusty nails from the boatyard days. They helped Lou drag rotten shingles down to the bank of the inlet.

"I'll haul out the garbage in my boat before Saturday," Lou told them.

They worked until just before dinnertime. Tim loaded Tyler and Dana's bikes into his truck and gave them a ride back to the Point.

"I'm seriously tired," Tyler said as they climbed the back steps of the lighthouse.

"And we've still got homework to do," Dana pointed out. "How long do you think we can keep this up?"

"For as long as it takes, I hope," said Tyler.

* * *

On Tuesday, they started painting the inside of the building. Even more Neptuners showed up, like Donny Nolan and Brian Wilson and Walter, and Luke Bucalo and another high-school kid named Alan. Cassie and Kim helped out, too.

By Wednesday, though, Tyler and Dana were dragging. Besides working at the Annex and keeping up with school stuff, they were busy at the stranding barn.

And Uncle Joe was getting seriously antsy about the birthday.

He cornered the cousins in the living room that evening and whispered, "Maybe a leisurely, dress-up dinner for the four of us in Wilton would be . . ."

Tyler and Dana looked at each other, and shook their heads.

"What's wrong with that?" Uncle Joe said. "We've only got three more days. I don't think you realize this is a serious situation!"

Then he peered closely at Dana, and said, "Hey, is that white paint in your hair?"

"Dad," Dana said in a low voice, "we have a story to tell you."

CHAPTER TWELVE

Dana had to give her dad credit—he managed to keep their secret. He told her mom they'd be taking her out to dinner in Wilton for her fortieth birthday, and left it at that.

And on Thursday afternoon, Joe Chapin showed up at the Annex himself and worked alongside Dana and Tyler, painting the walls a beautiful sea green.

On Friday, at least two dozen Neptuners helped out. Jane and Sue weren't there, though. They were busy planning the food for the party, along with the Willises, who owned the Lobster Inn in Rockport.

On Saturday, Dana and Tyler hung around the Point. They didn't want her mom to get suspicious with only hours to go! Then, late in the afternoon, they got dressed up for a birthday dinner at Belle Etoile, a fancy French restaurant in Wilton. The four of them climbed into their truck and headed into Rockport.

When they'd reached the curve at the far side of

town, Tyler suddenly blurted out, ''Oh, wow—I forgot! While we were getting ready, Tim Gilmore called. He found two big turtles at Wood Duck Inlet. . . .''

''And there's his truck,'' Dana's dad said smoothly, pointing out the window. ''We have plenty of time to get to the restaurant. Why don't I stop and see if Tim could use some help?''

He pulled onto the shoulder of the road. ''You three stay here, so you won't wreck your clothes. I'll be right back,'' he said.

Dana's mom said, ''Absolutely not—I'll go with you,'' which was exactly what they'd counted on her doing.

''Then we're coming, too,'' said Dana.

The four of them started down the trail toward the old boatyard. The sun had set, but there was still enough light left in the sky for them to dodge branches and stumps.

''I don't think I've ever been back here,'' Dana's mom said as they walked out into the clearing. ''I've certainly never seen this old building. . . .''

''The doors are open. Let's check it out,'' Tyler said loudly to Dana.

''Careful,'' Dana's mom said. She followed them through the doors, with Dana's dad a few steps behind her.

It was dark inside the building, and dead quiet. But Dana and Tyler walked quickly into the middle of the big room.

“Kids, where are you?” Dana’s mom asked, going more slowly.

“SURPRISE!” fifty or sixty voices shouted at once.

And suddenly rows of kerosene lanterns glowed brightly along the walls. Dana’s mom found herself standing in front of a long line of folding tables laden with food: fried shrimps and chicken, a roast turkey for sandwiches, potato salad, fruit salad, pineapple-orange punch.

In the center of the display, a huge birthday cake with a border of chocolate dolphins announced: “IT’S LISSA’S BIRTHDAY!”

Everybody was clapping and cheering. Almost all the adult Neptuners were there, along with Kim, Cassie, Hallie, and the Motes. Even Ms. Mercer had come to the party.

“I don’t believe this!” Lissa Chapin shrieked, while Dana and her dad gave her a big hug. “When did you have time to—”

“*Are* you surprised, Mom?” Dana asked over the racket.

“I’m absolutely stunned! How did you manage to keep it a secret?” said her mother. “And what is this place?”

Dana showed her a sign leaning against the near wall, with whales and dolphins frolicking among letters that rose like islands from a blue sea.

“Carter painted it,” Tyler said.

Lissa Chapin read aloud: “ ‘The Annex.’ ”

"It's ours now, so we'll never have to turn rescued animals away," Dana told her.

"*Ours?* But how . . ." her mom began.

"The kids did this," Dana's dad said. "And the Neptuners. And Ms. Mercer. The building belonged to her."

Ms. Mercer smiled from her place beside Sue Larkin and the Bucalos.

"It's a second home for Project Neptune," Joe Chapin went on, hugging Dana and Tyler. "I'm starving. Let's eat!"

AFTERWORD

Red tides occur all over the world, but they have nothing to do with tides. They're not always red, either, so scientists call them "harmful algal blooms," or HABs. Algal blooms are population explosions of microscopic, single-celled plants called algae. The blooms are usually brought on by warmer water temperatures and man-made pollution. Run-off from rainstorms and rivers washes chemicals and untreated sewage into the ocean, where they act as nutrients or fertilizers, causing algae to grow very fast. The tiny plants multiply by dividing: one cell becomes two, two become four, and so on. If conditions are right, a single alga can produce six thousand to eight thousand more cells in a week.

During a bloom, various kinds of harmful algae form dense patches near the surface of the ocean, sometimes red or brown, sometimes colorless. These algae are highly poisonous, clogging fishes' gills, paralyzing their breathing, and resulting in massive fish kills. The algae are also known to have killed dolphins, manatees—10 percent of the Florida manatee population died in 1996 as a result of an HAB—and even humpback whales.

If human beings eat certain types of fish affected by red tide, they might get severely nauseated, and experience muscle weakness and an irregular heartbeat. But the symptoms rarely last more than a few days. Shellfish like clams, oysters, and scallops, however, suck the algae into their bodies while they're feeding, and the poison builds up in their flesh. They become so toxic that a single clam can kill the person who eats it. Symptoms of paralytic shellfish poisoning (PSP) can appear quickly, within ten minutes: drowsiness, tingling, shortness of breath, a choking feeling, slurred speech, and rapid pulse. Soon the victim's chest becomes paralyzed, he can't breathe on his own, and without medical assistance he can die within twelve hours.

Algal poisons found in ocean water, and airborne droplets in sea spray, are much less dangerous, but they can cause coughing, sneezing, difficulty in breathing, stinging eyes, and skin rashes.

Scientists are trying to come up with methods to control red tides—for example, common clay in liquid or powdered form has been used in Asia in an effort to stop blooms. But the most obvious way to discourage red tides is to cut down on the man-made pollutants that wash into our oceans.

For an illustration of the life cycle of a single algal cell, visit:

http://www.redtide.whoi.edu/hab/whathabs/whathabs.html

For photos and satellite imaging of red tide blooms, as well as microphotographs of harmful algae, visit:

http://www.redtide.whoi.edu/hab/rtphotos/rtphotos.html

For a photograph of a fish kill in Florida resulting from an HAB, visit:

http://www.redtide.whoi.edu/hab/foodweb/fishkills.html